ELLA MEETS WILLY WOLF AT THE ZOO

Ian Samson

This is a work of fiction. Names, characters, places and incidents
either are the product of the author's imagination or are used
fictitiously, and any resemblance to any actual persons, living or
dead, events, or locales is entirely coincidental.

To order additional copies of this book, contact:
Xlibris
NZ TFN: 0800 008 756 (Toll Free inside the NZ)
NZ Local: 9-801 1905 (+64 9801 1905 from outside New Zealand)
www.xlibris.co.nz
Orders@ Xlibris.co.nz

ISBN: Softcover   978-1-5434-9714-4
          EBook   978-1-5434-9713-7

Print information available on the last page

Rev. date: 06/25/2021

Ella Meets Willy Wolf

at the Zoo

"Hello, Mummy. Hello, Daddy. I am awake now," says Ella.

"Good morning, Ella," says Mummy.

"We have a surprise for you, Ella. Today we are going to the zoo!" says Daddy.

Ella is very excited, so she jumps out of bed to get ready for the zoo.

Mummy, Daddy, and Ella arrive at the zoo. It is very busy.

After they buy their tickets, they walk towards a big gate at the entrance to the zoo that says "Welcome Everyone." Ella squeals with excitement.

As Ella walks around the zoo, she sees many lovely animals.

Ella laughs when she sees the monkeys swinging by their tails.

"They're playing games in the trees," says Daddy.

6

Ella then sees a very big camel. It has a big hump on its back and long legs.

"Her name is Alice," says Mummy. Ella laughs.

Next, Ella sees a very tall giraffe.

The giraffe is so tall that it can almost reach the sky.

As Ella waves hello, the giraffe comes over to the fence to say hi to Ella.

Finally, Ella sees a big hairy wolf. She has never seen a wolf before.

"Is that a big dog, Daddy?" she asks.

"No. That's a big wolf," says Daddy. "It looks like a dog, but it's bigger, stronger, and has very sharp teeth. It lives in the wild."

The wolf's name is Willy Wolf. He is very friendly and comes over to Ella to play.

Willy Wolf wags his tail and jumps up and down.

Ella thinks Willy Wolf is the best animal in the zoo.

Mummy, Daddy, and Ella then go and get an ice cream.

"Yummy!" says Ella as she licks her ice cream.

Oops! Ella's ice cream falls off the cone. Ella feels sad.

"It's OK to feel sad, Ella," says Mummy, "but don't worry; we'll get you a new one."

"Thank you, Mummy," says Ella.

After a long day at the zoo, it is time to go home.

Ella waves goodbye to Willy Wolf.

"Goodbye, Willy Wolf. I love you," she says.

Willy Wolf wags his tail to say goodbye.

When they get home, Ella asks, "Can we go back to the zoo tomorrow to see Willy Wolf?"

"Maybe," Daddy says, "but only if you are a good girl."

That night, Ella has a lovely dream about Willy Wolf at the zoo. She knows she has made a new friend and can't wait to go visit him again.

THE END

CPSIA information can be obtained
at www.ICGtesting.com
Printed in the USA
LVHW070137070721
691975LV00001B/39